Anonymous

Poems of Nantucket

Anonymous

Poems of Nantucket

ISBN/EAN: 9783337397982

Printed in Europe, USA, Canada, Australia, Japan

Cover: Foto ©Andreas Hilbeck / pixelio.de

More available books at **www.hansebooks.com**

I know an isle, clasped in the sea's strong arms,
Sport of his rage and sharer of his dreams;
A barren spot to alien eyes it seems,
But for its own it wears unfading charms.
From Spring's first kiss to Autumn's last caress,
Gayly its moorlands bloom from strand to strand,
And many a favored nook by west winds fanned,
Holds flowers unmatched for tint and loveliness.

From "Cactus," by EMILY S. FORMAN

. . .

NANTUCKET

PUBLISHED BY HENRY S. WYER.

1888.

INDEX.

POEMS OF NANTUCKET.

FROM "THE EXILES," 1660.*

BY JOHN G. WHITTIER.

THEY passed the gray rocks of Cape Ann,
 And Gloucester's harbor bar :
The watch-fire of the garrison
 Shone like a setting star.

How brightly broke the morning
 On Massachusetts Bay !
Blue wave, and bright green island,
 Rejoicing in the day.

On passed the bark in safety
 Round isle and headland steep ;
No tempest broke above them,
 No fog-cloud veiled the deep.

* By permission of Houghton, Mifflin & Co.

Far round the bleak and stormy cape
  The vent'rous Macey passed.
And on Nantucket's naked isle
  Drew up his boat at last.

And how, in log-built cabin.
  They braved the rough sea weather;
And there, in peace and quietness.
  Went down life's vale together.

How others drew around them.
  And how their fishing sped.
Until to every wind of heaven
  Nantucket's sails were spread.

How pale Want alternated
  With Plenty's golden smile;
Behold, is it not written
  In the annals of the Isle?

And yet that Isle remaineth
  A refuge of the free,
As when true-hearted Macey
  Beheld it from the sea.

Free as the winds that winnow
    Her shrubless hills of sand,
Free as the waves that batter
    Along her yielding land.

Than hers. at duty's summons.
    No loftier spirit stirs.
Nor falls o'er human suffering
    A readier tear than hers.

God bless the sea-beat island !
    And grant forevermore
That charity and freedom dwell
    As now. upon her shore '

A THOUSAND YEARS AGO.

BY REV. PHEBE A. HANAFORD.

ALMOST a thousand years ago
   The Norseman's venturous keel
Ploughed from the icy-island bays
   And found, for woe or weal,
The land we call our native isle,
   The harbors that we know :
They looked upon Nantucket's shores
   A thousand years ago.

Almost a thousand years ago,
   Where now our steamer plies,
Waved in the breeze the yellow hair,
   And gleamed the azure eyes
Of those who won the Viking's fame
   While sailing to and fro,
With steadfast scorn of hardships here,
   A thousand years ago.

POEMS OF NANTUCKET.

Almost a thousand years ago
   They traced their watery way.
Far off beheld the island rise
   From out the white-capped sea,
And watched the breakers, foaming, dash
   Upon the shores we know, —
Those dauntless men of brave renown!
   A thousand years ago.

Almost a thousand years ago
   They saw the bluff of sand,
Where now we see the beacon light
   Far flash o'er sea and land,
They dreamed not of the mighty march
   Of mind and life we know,
Who read each page, unwritten then,
   A thousand years ago.

Almost a thousand years ago,
   Yet history tells, sublime,
The tale of old Nantucket's life
   In that millennial time:

And we who, on this distant day,
Are proud that tale to know.
Rejoice that hardy voyagers came
A thousand years ago!

New Haven, Conn., Nov. 1, 1887.

NANTUCKET MOORS.

BY CAROLINE PARKER HILLS.

HERE are pines for perfume,
    Golden-rods and fern ;
Briers, with their berries,
    That like the ruby burn :
Meadow larks for music,
    Fluttering to their nest :
'Mid the grass and heather
    Sit we here to rest.

Here are lakes for brightness,
    Wondrous in their hue :
Fairy lakes sequestered,
    With only me and you.
On the wing are sea-gulls :
    The hawk soars high for prey :
In the sedgy hollows
    The marsh wren hides away.

You and I for comrades,
  On heath so weird and wild :
Ocean billows surging,
  Where sunset clouds are piled.
How each path enchanted
  Woos us to return.
Scented with the brier
  And perfumed with the fern !

List the dwarf pine sighing,
  Here the larks complain !
'T is the hour of parting,
  And parting means but pain.
Farewell, bird and blossom !
  Farewell. flower and vine !
Ah ! what grief to sever
  Such hearts as mine and thine !

SONNETS.

BY EMILY SHAW FORMAN.

CACTUS.

(PRICKLY PEAR.)

I KNOW an isle, clasped in the sea's strong arms,
Sport of his rage, and sharer of his dreams;
A barren spot to alien eyes it seems.
But for its own it wears unfading charms.
From Spring's first kiss to Autumn's last caress.
Gayly its moorlands bloom from strand to strand.
And many a favored nook by west winds fanned
Holds flowers unmatched for tint and loveliness.
But most I mind me of a lonesome shore,
For countless gulls a harbor and freehold.
Where, like some shipwrecked buccaneer of old.
Cast on the sands, condemned to roam no more,
In spiny armature secure and bold,
The Cactus lies at length, and guards its gold.

* *Opuntia vulgaris* reaches its farthest northern limit at Nantucket

BEACH-PLUM.

LIKE childhood's smile, half trusting, half afraid,
  A thought of Spring steals o'er the landscape's face,
Told in the slender wind-flower's lissome grace,
Breathed from the Arbutus, that loves the shade.
Writ in the deep'ning blue of sea and sky.
And look! where, whipt by winds from east and north.
The sturdy beach-plum puts her blossoms forth, —
A wonder of white beauty to the eye,
A sphinx half buried in the shifting sand.
I would thy pretty riddle I could guess,
Of prudent thrift that looks like lavishness,
Of Autumn fruitage in chill Springtime planned.
Or learn by what rare craft, what hidden hands,
Thou hoardest ruby wine from these salt sands.

HUDSONIA.

NOT in the cloistered safety of the woods,
  Where the fair firstlings of the Springtime hide,
Not the gay, laughing, dancing brook beside,
Nor in the hush of mountain solitudes,
Seek we for thee, O hardy pioneer!
Upon the barren, bleak, and wind-swept sand
Of sea-girt isles thy feet are set.   There, fanned
By breezes salt with spray, thou dost not fear
To spread thy couch of velvet tapestry,
With golden flowers soon to be 'broidered o'er.
A new Canute, thou sittest on the shore,
Sending brave challenge to the mighty sea :
While, far and near, as waiting thy command,
The glist'ning ranks of sturdy beach-grass stand.

PURPLE GERARDIA.

IN that fair, dreamy border land, that lies
   Between the glowing zone of Summer flowers, —
Frail, fleet recorders of the summer hours, —
And Autumn's belt of gold and purple dyes.
O my Gerardia, thou reignest queen.
Tribute from both thou gatherest, I think,
Since thy right royal robe of purple pink
Holds tints of June in its rich, rosy sheen,
Deepened with touch of Autumn hues to come.
So, too, a pleasing sadness marks thy reign.
A Summer joy, dashed with presage of pain :
For when o'er dale and down flushes thy bloom.
We sadly smile, to think thy pretty bells
Must toll the dying Summer's passing knells.

ALEC. DUNHAM'S BOAT.

BY CHARLES HENRY WEBB.

THERE she lies at her moorings.
  The little two-master,
Answering not now
  The call of disaster.
Loose swings the rudder,
  Unshipped the tiller —
Crossing the Bar so,
  One sea would fill her!

Foresail and mainsail
  In loose folds are lying;
Naked the mast-heads —
  No pennon flying:
Sea-weed and wreck
  Alike may drift past her;
Here lies the pilot-boat —
  Where is her master?

Lantern at Great Point.
　Brightly it burns:
Beacon on Brant Point
　The signal returns.
Far out to sea
　Sankoty flashes:
White on the shore
　The crested wave dashes.

Strident No'theaster
　And smoky Sou'wester
Call for the pilot-boat,
　Eager to test her.
And a ship on the Bar,
　Just where the waves cast her!
Moored lies the pilot-boat —
　Where is her master?

Oh, bark driving in,
　God send that you lee get,
Past Tuckernuck shoals,
　The reefs of Muskeget.

There go minute-guns :
    Now faster and faster —
But no more to their aid
    Flies the little two-master.

For the pilot one night
    Left his boat as you see her —
Light moored, that at signal
    He ready might free her.
But not from her moorings
    Came the pilot to cast her,
Though a signal he answered —
    One set by the Master

Gone, say you, and whither?
    Do you ask me which way
Went good pilot as ever
    Brought ship into bay !
Who shall say how he cast off,
    If to starboard or larboard?
But of one thing I 'm sure —
    The pilot's safe harbored !

NANTUCKET, DEC. 3, 1881

THE HOUSE-TOP WALK.

BY CHARLES L. THOMPSON.

WEATHER-STAINED and beaten and empty now,
 The long, long vigil o'er;
No longer the ships go out to sea,
 And the watchers wait no more;
Sailors and watchers are resting now,
 Some on this sandy lea,
And some with the sea-grass round them twined,
 Are asleep in the wandering sea.

But it comes to me as I walk the street
 Of the quaint, historic town,
A vision these scenes have looked upon
 In the years so long agone, —
A vision of struggle with storm and tide,
 By the brave ones, called to roam
On the wrathful way of the ocean wide;
 And a vision of love at home.

On the house-top walk in the morning gray.
  And yet in the deepening night,
They watch for the flash of a homeward sail,
  Or the swing of a mast-head light.
It is morn again, and again 't is eve,
  So the days drag one by one,
And the steadfast thing in the changeful scene
  Is the love that will have its own.

So the hair grows gray, and the faces thin,
  For the sea is empty still:
And the lonely years will have their way,
  And God will have His will.
But the watch is o'er.   What matters now
  Though the ships drift endlessly,
Though some are asleep in the graveyard there
  And some in the wandering sea?

THE ETERNAL ATLANTIC.

BY REV. PHEBE A. HANAFORD.

THE sandy beach still stretches wide and far.
  And, wondrous still, and free,
Outreaches to the dim horizon's verge
  The vast and lonely sea.

White sails may dot its blue waves on those days
  When all is calm and light;
And white clouds in their spiral beauty rise
  From steamers just in sight.

But by the starlight, and in moonlight hour,
  The ocean seems so lone,
The wide, vast, throbbing, and eternal sea —
  Its voice become a moan.

Not so, when on the beach the bathers throng,
  And strength and beauty lend
Their wide attraction to the healthful joy
  In which the hour they spend.

Then, with exultant bound, the swimmer seeks
   The bright, pulsating sea,
And on its buoyant waters calmly floats,
   Or breasts its billowy glee.

Changes may come : old homesteads pass from those
   Whose early days they blessed ;
And many a loved one soar from earthly paths
   To share the heavenly rest.

But still the sea remains, and on its breast
   The sunshine sparkles fair,
While happy children on its borders play,
   And lovers wander there.

And when the moonbeams make their path of light
   To touch the echoing shore,
Fond eyes gaze on the glorious beauty there,
   Nor heed the breakers' roar.

Forever, then, will mortal seek this isle,
   Whose shores that ocean laves,
Upon whose bosom her brave sons were kings,
   And in their realm no slaves.

Eternal waters ! lave those shores so dear,
  And health and strength impart
To those who seek the peace that Nature gives
The true and noble heart.

NEW HAVEN, CONN.. MIDSUMMER DAY, 1885.

SEA MOSSES

BY ANNA GARDNER

YE tiny wanderers of the trackless sea.
  Ye rainbow-tinted treasures of the deep.
Borne on the rising tide, how tranquilly
Ye rest on waves that ever landward sweep.
Or on old ocean's mane in joyous gambols leap'

As on your vari-colored forms we gaze,
How busy fancy wakens sea dreams rare!
All floating in imagination's haze
Are graceful mermaids twining flow'rets fair
With glit'ring shells and stones, to deck their golden h

Piercing its cavern'd depths, bold fancy's eye
Wanders along the sea's mosaic floor,
Studded with pearls and shells of richest dye,
With sparkling gems and trophies scattered o'er,
Which to their ocean beds the native sea-nymphs bore

Ye graceful types of treasures bright. concealed
In caverned chambers of the mighty deep,
In vasty solitudes, where, unrevealed
To mortal sight, fair nymphs their vigils keep
O'er many a form wreathed for its last, long sleep.

Symbols of thoughts in scattered fragments tossed
Upon the heaving surface of the mind,
From its profoundest depths unfathomed. lost
In an unbounded scope where, undefined,
In the mind's starry chambers, wisdom dwells enshrined.

ON THE PASSAGE OF THE CONSTITUTIONAL AMENDMENT.

BY ANNA GARDNER.

TO-DAY God smiles upon our cause :
  The nation's heart beats high !
To-day, the heaven-defying laws
  (Accursed) of slavery
Are blotted from our nation's page
  By Freedom's royal hand,
While grateful, throbbing hearts presage
  Peace to our war-worn land.

The shackles from four million slaves
  Fall, broken, to the ground :
Our starry banner proudly waves,
  Our bells exultant sound :
From town to town, from sea to sea,
  By loyal breezes fanned,
The joyous peal of liberty
  Rings out through all the land.

The freedman, kneeling on the soil,
  Bedewed with tears and blood
Wrung out by unrequited toil,
  Breaks forth in praise to God.
His long, long life of agony,
  And concentrated wrong,
Exchanged for rapt'rous liberty,
  Oh, raise the grateful song !

Peal upon peal, let heartfelt thanks
  Salute the ambient air :
No chain throughout the South land clanks,
  No blood-stained scourge is there.
From north to south, from east to west,
  Swell high the loud acclaim !
Dark slavery's curse no more shall rest
  Upon our nation's fame !

Thank God ! our country now is free,
  Redeemed from slavery's blight.
Ring out, O joy bells, merrily,
  Ring in an age of light.

Triumphant let the shout be heard.
  " Freedom for coming years ! "
While distant nations catch the word.
  And echo back our cheers.

NANTUCKET SURF-SIDE.

BY CAROLINE PARKER HILLS.

A VARYING coast. with smoothly shining sand.
   A surf that breaks in thunder on the shore.
Where Neptune's coursers. racing toward the land.
   Wave their white manes amid the ocean's roar.

From far-off lands what tidings bring ye here.
   Ye waves, that hither speed with giant surge?
What vessel have ye wrecked, in wild career?
   What tell ye of the stranded seaman's dirge?

With shuddering crest of rainbow hues, erect.
   Poised for an instant, chafing in mid-air.
A crash replies, and all the beach is flecked
   With iridescent foam, spread like a snare ;

Or like the sparkling jewels of a crown
   That some fair mermaid flings from pearly caves,
Herself safe hidden countless fathoms down,
   The joyous plaything of the winds and waves.

What tales of buried treasure couldst thou tell,
    Resistless sea, so mighty in thy wrath !
What cargoes of the Orient, with a knell
    Of anguish, merged beneath the storm-king's path !

On this lone cliff, that holds the floods at bay,
    Perchance some youthful lovers may have sate,
And watched the heaving billows fling their spray,
    In golden moments snatched from bitter fate.

For he to distant shores has steered his bark,
    While she is left, to count the lonely hours ;
To dream of him each day from dawn till dark,
    And gather in life's thistles, not its flowers.

O sea ! forbear such faithful hearts to rend !
    Wreck not their hopes, though far the wand'rer roam :
Ye watery sprites, to him your magic lend,
    And waft him safely to his island home.

WHEN THE SEA GREW WHITE.

IN THE GREAT GALE, OCT. 12, 1878.

BY ARTHUR ELWELL JENKS.

SWEETLY it rose o'er our Island town,
 The October moon ; while never a frown
Crossed the brow of the evening sky,
Or shadowed the dreadful storm so nigh !
Bright and tender the white moonlight,
Who would have read one token of fright
In all the peace of that harvest scene?
No prophecy, save of rest, I ween.
I heard not the whispers that shook the trees,
Nor heeded the dirge of the wailing breeze.

On gray old Sankoty's rugged height
The starry hosts seemed to smile that night :
The sea below, in an undertone,
Lay chanting its melody, all alone.

I did not read in the sea, or air,
Or in quivering leaflet, anywhere.
The mystic sign of the awful gale,
At thought of which my cheek turns pale !
The harbor lights, and Great Point's eye,
With friendly glance, gleamed steadily,
And ever the bell-buoy rose and fell,
With the lazy dip of the ocean's swell.
From the blazing vines and scarlet heath,
Where mild October twines her wreath,
Came the breath of pine boughs, Autumn's tide
Of trailing glories — Nantucket's pride.

But something I saw, that crossed the moon,
Seemed an omen of storm which would startle me soon
For afar, in his northern lair, there lay
A monster cloud, like a fiend at bay.
But why did I dread, as never before,
The sound of the waves on the sullen shore?
I cannot tell.   But I heard, alone,
The voice of a wrath I dared not own ;
And at morning's dawn I saw the sky
Look out with a wild and threat'ning eye.

Over the harbor bar the spray
Blinded the mariner all that day.
And the rain came on, like the flood of old.
With the desolate moan of a wintry wold.
The roofs and towers of the ancient town
Grew black with the dark mist swooping down :
All day it surged. like a tidal wave.
And the hearts of the people, so true and brave.
Beat quick with fear. Down came the night.
With never a star. and the sea was white !

O wives and mothers. so far away,
God temper the grief of this fatal day.
When the twain were drowned 'neath the frowning bluff
Of Sankoty's headland — it was sad enough.
Where Muskeget's channel cleaves its way.
Just out of our Island's peaceful bay.
A captain's wife, himself and crew.
All lost, with the friendly land in view.
Save one ; he survived. the tale to tell ;
(Thanksgiving for those who loved him well!)
But 'Sconset saw a cruel sight :
The mocking rage of the " Old Man's " might :

Stood, and beheld within their reach,
Beyond the surf of the long Low Beach,
A sinking vessel — " God pity the men ! "
The terrible shoal devouring them then,
And many a craft, with a tattered sail,
Went down in the merciless wave and gale :
And many a man was lost that night,
With never a star, when the sea grew white !

"ROUND CAPE HORN."

S. L.

ASK any question in this town,
　　Of any one, by night or morn.
The answer will be always found,
　　　　　　　　　" Round Cape Horn."

I ask the ladies where I call,
　　" Your husbands, are they here or gone?"
And get this answer from them all, —
　　　　　　　　　" Round Cape Horn."

I asked a child I chanced to meet,
　　" Where is your pa, my dear, this morn?"
She answered with a smile most sweet, —
　　　　　　　　　" Round Cape Horn."

I asked a boy as on he skipped,
　　" Where now, my lad, at early dawn?"
He answered (for he then had shipped), —
　　　　　　　　　" Round Cape Horn."

POEMS OF NANTUCKET

I asked an aged man one day.
   How time had passed since he was born.
" My years," said he, " have passed away.
              · Round Cape Horn.' "

I asked a sailor bound away,
   Where I should write when he was gone.
He said without the least delay, —
              " Round Cape Horn."

I asked a merchant for a fee.
   He turned and answered me with scorn,
" My property is all at sea,
             · Round Cape Horn.' "

I then to a mechanic went.
   And he likewise bade me begone,
For all he had, and more, was sent
            " Round Cape Horn."

I asked a sister whom I saw.
   Quite finely dressed in silks and lawn,
" Where 's your brother?" She answered, " La !
           · Round Cape Horn.' "

I asked a maiden by my side,
   Who sighed and looked to me forlorn,
" Where is your heart?"   She quick replied, —
              " Round Cape Horn."

I asked a widow why she cried,
   As she sat lonely taking on :
She said her husband lately died,
              " Round Cape Horn."

I asked a mother of the dead
   From whom support she long had drawn,
" Where did he die?"   She merely said, —
              " Round Cape Horn."

I said, " I 'll let your fathers know,"
   To boys in mischief on the lawn ;
They all replied, " Then you must go
              · Round Cape Horn.'"

I asked a loafer idling round,
   If he would work : when, with a yawn,
He answered, " No! till I am bound
              · Round Cape Horn.'"

In fact, I asked a little boy,
    If he could tell where he was born ;
He answered with a mark of joy,
                        " Round Cape Horn.

There 's scarce a thing I chance to see
    Brought here, the Island to adorn.
But either was, or soon will be,
                        " Round Cape Horn

Thus merchants, sailors, women, men,
    The old, or children lately born,
To all you ask, reply again, —
                        " Round Cape Horn.

Now you who know, an answer give,
    Do I stay here, or am I gone?
Tell me if I do surely live
                        " Round Cape Horn.

                    * A fact.

TACKING SHIP OFF SHORE.

BY REV. WALTER MITCHELL.

THE weather leach of the topsail shivers,
 The bow lines strain, and the lee shrouds slacken.
The braces are taut and the lithe boom quivers,
 And the waves with the coming squall-cloud blacken.

Open one point on the weather bow
 Is the lighthouse tall on Fire Island head :
There 's a shade of doubt on the captain's brow.
 And the pilot watches the heaving lead.

I stand at the wheel, and with eager eye
 To sea, and to sky, and to shore I gaze,
Till the muttered order of " FULL AND BY !"
 Is suddenly changed to " FULL FOR STAYS !"

The ship bends lower before the breeze,
 As her broadside fair to the blast she lays :
And she swifter springs to the rising seas
 As the pilot calls, " STAND BY FOR STAYS !"

It is silence all, as each in his place,
  With the gathered coils in his hardened hands,
By tack and bow line, by sheet and brace,
  Waiting the watchword, impatient stands.

And the light on Fire Island head draws near,
  As, trumpet-winged, the pilot's shout
From his post on the bowsprit's heel I hear,
  With the welcome call of " READY ! ABOUT !"

No time to spare ! it is touch-and-go,
  And the captain growls, " DOWN HELM ! HARD DOWN !"
As my weight on the whirling spokes I throw,
  While heaven grows black with the storm-cloud's frown

High o'er the knight-heads flies the spray,
  As we meet the shock of the plunging sea :
And my shoulder stiff to the wheel I lay,
  As I answer, " AY, AY, SIR ! HARD A LEE !"

With the swerving leap of a startled steed,
  The ship flies fast in the eye of the wind,
The dangerous shoals on the lee recede,
  And the headland white we have left behind.

The topsails flutter, the jibs collapse,
    And belly and tug at the groaning cleats ;
The spanker slaps and the mainsail flaps,
    And thunders the order, " TACKS AND SHEETS ! "

'Mid the rattle of blocks and the tramp of the crew,
    Hisses the rain of the rushing squall ;
The sails are aback from clew to clew,
    And now is the moment for " MAINSAIL HAUL ! "

And the heavy yards, like a baby's toy,
    By fifty strong arms are swiftly swung :
She holds her way, and I look with joy
    For the first white spray o'er the bulwarks flung.

" LET GO AND HAUL ! " 't is the last command,
    And the head-sails fill to the blast once more ;
Astern and to leeward lies the land,
    With its breakers white on the shingly shore.

What matters the reef, or the rain, or the squall?
    I steady the helm for the open sea ;
The first mate clamors, " BELAY THERE ALL ! "
    And the captain's breath once more comes free.

And so off shore let the good ship fly.
  Little care I how the gusts may blow ;
In my fo'castle bunk, in a jacket dry,
  Eight bells have struck, and my watch is below

THE BUOY-BELL

BY B. J. LEEDOM.

THE mournful tone of the Buoy-Bell
  Is sweeping across the wave;
Like a solemn dirge, or a funeral knell
  O'er some mariner's watery grave.

The sea-gull screams, as it circles around,
  And poises in upper air,
As it lists to the clang of its doleful sound,
  Like the wailing cry of despair.

And often at night, when the wind is low,
  And the billows have ceased their roar,
The Buoy-Bell, rocking to and fro,
  Is heard on the distant shore.

The mother awakes from her troubled sleep,
  When she hears it sound on the air;
And fears for the loved ones far on the deep,
  Whilst her thoughts are ascending in prayer.

And the fond wife starts from her peaceful rest,
    As she hears its midnight cry:
And clasps her babe more close to her breast,
    As its mournful song sweeps by.

'Tis the Buoy-Bell! 'tis the Buoy-Bell!
    As it falls on the mariner's ear,
Its ringing tone in sweet accents tell
    Of the home he is drawing near:

And he pauses oft, in his lonely round,
    When the bright stars gleam on high;
And firmly grasps his helm at the sound,
    As his vessel glides safely by.

There 's a Buoy-Bell heard in every soul,
    A warning that sounds within,
That will ever guide from the dangerous shoal,
    And quicksand that covereth sin.

A still small voice in the cool of the day,
    When the cares of the world are at rest,
If mortals would heed its pure, gentle sway,
    Would lead to a haven of rest.

There 's a Buoy-Bell sounding in every heart ;
    If we heeded its warning tone,
"T would lead us to choose that better part,
    And commune with God alone.

"T is simply to trust in a Father's hand.
    Who doeth all things well,
Who can safely guide to the promised land
    By the inward Buoy-Bell.

NANTUCKET CLIFF.

BY CAROLINE PARKER HILLS.

HIGH on a cliff, o'erlooking land and sea,
   A cottage, vine-clad, woos the summer skies :
The robins freely give their minstrelsy,
   The meadow-lark from hidden covert flies.

The hay-fields, ripening, waft their fragrant breath,
   In verdant contrast with the sea's vast deep :
And here the farmer gleans the after-math,
   And there the white-sailed shallops glide or sleep.

How silver-toned the distant village bell,
   That rings the matin and the vesper chime.
Like blissful dream, the lingering sounds that tell
   The onward flight of swift eluding time.

O days so brightly blest, so ample crowned !
   O nights, where ocean breezes blandly play !
Could way-worn pilgrim better shrine have found
   Than where the sea-tern takes her devious way?

Though storms ere long may dark above them lower,
    Yet He who guides the bird through mist and foam
Will not forget to shelter with His power
    The happy dwellers in their island home.

A PICTURE.

BY ANNA C. STARBUCK.

OVER the road to 'Sconset.
  That dear old, sea-blown place.
The dreamy fisher-hamlet,
  Where smiles the ocean's face ;
Over the road to 'Sconset
  I 'm riding all alone ;
And the sunset's sweet reflections
  Are warmly akin to my own.

Alone, save the grim old driver,
  Who sits on the forward seat.
Lazily jerking his pony,
  And leaving my silence complete.
I nestle far back in the corner,
  Am reckoned asleep by his chart,
But 't is summer-tide over the moorland,
  And summer is flooding my heart.

Asleep?   I am reading the poem
    That Nature is shimmering down :
I am quaffing each delicate odor
    That comes from the heather brown ;
I am answering the eyes of the mosses
    That peer with a welcoming grace
Up from their sandy roadway.
    In search of my happy face.

I am noting the stretch of the " commons,"
    The prairie-like roll of the land :
I care not to number the mile-stones.
    That flaunt me their faces so bland.
No monotone burdens the journey.
    Each wheel turns a fresh internode.
For I love every inch of the distance.
    Each sod and each rut of the road.

There 's a breath from the sea, a-quiver
    With health and new guerdon of life ;
And my heart to the heart of the Giver
    Is throbbing with gratitude. rife.

So over the road to 'Sconset
   I 'm riding all alone ;
And the sunset's sweet reflections
   Are warmly akin to my own.

SHARING FOSTER'S FATE.

BY ANNA C. STARBUCK.

ONE Christmas night — so runs the story old —
  A sailor's wife sat list'ning to the roar
Of breakers, and the chafing of the wind
That creaked the hinges of her cottage door;
And thinking of her husband far away,
Her simple heart grew anxious for its mate,
Till, conning o'er her early marriage vow
To share with him the suns and storms of fate,
Her reckless mind o'erleaped her reason's bounds :
She tied a snowy kerchief on her head,
And, flinging wide the window's icy sash,
She leaned her feeble body out, and said :
" Dear Foster, it is stormy, cold, and late,
But here am I to share your cruel fate ! "

That very hour, beneath a southern sun,
Old Foster sat, contented with his life ;

His selfish nature revelled in the scene.
Nor gave one thought unto his simple wife.
His taut old ship at anchor rose and fell.
Responsive to the surging of the tide :
While spicy odors from the ripening fruits
Mixed softly with the breeze on every side.
He pared an orange lazily, and said.
" Returning winds our waiting sails shall spread.
From this, methinks, a lesson may be borne :
What need to fret and fume away the hours?
For though the storm may fright us with its roar
The choicest hidden blessings may be ours
'T is weak to borrow trouble, and be led
By phantoms, since our Father 's overhead.

MOONLIGHT.

BY MARTHA HUSSEY LAMBERTON.

ACROSS the ocean streams a flood of light,
   Huge waves, aglow with brightness, rise and fall;
A wondrous beauty clothes the peaceful night,
   As soft the moonbeams glisten over all;
From out the dark, where dashing breakers roar,
   One silver path creeps downward to our feet;
It sparkles, trembles, dimples to the shore,
   And stretches far, where sky and wavelets meet.

Upon life's sea of surging human woes
   A glory shines, though dark the night and drear;
Before each soul a silver pathway glows —
   A path of duty, radiant and clear.
We cannot see another's guide, nor view
   The whole grand glory flash from shore to shore;
One tender gleam shines ever calm and true,
   And leads to rest and peace forevermore.

THE "SCHOOL-HOUSE ON THE HILL."

BY WM. HUSSEY MACY.

PEAL loud the bell, and call the school together!
   We are but " children of a larger growth."
Though now, matured, we range with longer tether,
   Restraints and duties appertain to both
Childhood and manhood — parts of life's progression —
Peal loud the bell! the school's again in session!

And as we meet to-day, on classic ground,
   To enjoy and celebrate our great Reunion,
To let the story, song, and jest go round,
   To call up bygones, and, in glad communion,
To interchange experiences of life,
Of wanderings and trials, toil and strife.

Let us awhile, with retrospective view,
   Go back to eighteen hundred thirty-eight,
When what is now the *old* school was the *new*,
   Not having yet sent forth a graduate.

Impressed on mem'ry's page, we see it still,
The venerable " School-house on the Hill."

We see again each sturdy little " form,"
    Painted in *ridicule* of bird's-eye maple,
The clumsy stoves, which failed to keep us warm,
    The drinking-closet door, with hook and staple.
The little room, enclosing various matters,
Labelled conspicuously. " Apparatus."

The staring figures. blazoned on the seats,
    The pegs for hats, numbered to correspond.
The bell-rope, leading down between its cleats,
    The windows, looking on the " Lily Pond,"
The maps. the black-boards fixed against the wall,
All rise before us now, at mem'ry's call.

Then Father Pierce reigned over us, who seemed,
    To us, a cyclopædia of knowledge ;
Not less for humble piety esteemed
    Than for his stores of learning, gained at college :
We think of him as teacher, guide, and pastor —
A faithful servant of the greater Master.

And after him, our veteran teacher, Morse,
　Who, more than others, made the school his own
By long and arduous service in its cause,
　Giving to it his spirit and his tone,
And grafting his own character upon us, —
He lives to-day to wear his well-earned honors.

The pupils of the *old* school on the hill
　Are scattered broadcast — some have passed away,
But others, spared to do it honor still,
　May, with their children, gather here to-day :
Two generations, vying with each other
In love and tribute to their *one* Fair Mother.

A fine new school-house has usurped the old :
　Yet " on the Hill " it stands, a beacon light,
Shedding its rays, more precious far than gold,
　And younger pupils now may claim the right
To pen its later hist'ry, and to tell
How other teachers labored, and how well.

Let then the new-made High School graduate
　Take up the Book of Chronicles anew,
As we about the *old* school love to prate,
　So let the young Alumni sing the *new*.

One theme may both inspire : it stands there still,
Ever the same — the " School-house on the Hill."

Long may it stand ! its " shadow ne'er grow less " !
   Our children, and our children's children may,
In years to come, rejoice in its success,
   And sing its praises ; let us ever pray
For blessings on it, and, with hearty will,
Cherish for aye the " School-house on the Hill."

REUNION ANTHEM.

Air, " America."

BY MRS. ELIZABETH STARBUCK.

OUR native Isle! of thee
  With voices loud and free,
Praises we'll sing;
Let children's children come
To their ancestral home,
Wreathed by the deep sea's foam,
  And tribute bring!

Our fathers bless'd thy soil:
Those hardy sons of toil
  Found refuge here
Upon thine unbroke sod,
From persecution's rod
That bath'd the earth in blood,
  The heart in fear.

Their light as diff'ring star
Shineth, still gleams afar
  To guide us on :
In learning's sacred bower
It glads with magic power,
And youth's gay, sunny hour
  Is rife with song.

Bright, golden skies are thine,
Rich flowers, the clust'ring vine,
  The outstretch'd plain ;
Thy waters murmuring low,
Or surging as they flow
Wild waves in grandeur go,
  And loud refrain.

Welcome, ye kinsmen dear !
Welcome, thou stranger here
  Within our gates !
Ye cherished, absent ones !
As shade of sadness comes
Love hears your echoing tones,
  Your presence waits.

In this communion sweet
Hands clasp: hearts are replete
   With joy — with pain:
Our lov'd, with voices hush'd.
Strengthen faith in the trust,
" That somewhere meet we must "
   And live again.

Good bye! ye loving hearts
Good bye! the tear-drop starts
   To say good bye!
The mem'ries of the day
Shall linger 'round our way
Long after we shall say
   Good bye! good bye!

TRISTRAM AND DIONIS COFFIN, NANTUCKET.

An Acrostic. A visit (in imagination) to Portledge Manor.

BY M. F. ALLEN.

TOWARDS Devonshire I turn my feet.
   Resolved the ancestral home to see.
In hopes some kinsman there to meet.
   Some scion of our ancient tree.
The hearty welcome there I met
   Revived my heart, my strength renewed:
And time shall cease ere I forget
   My joy as I the prospect viewed.
As Portledge Place before me stood,
   No language can my thoughts convey :
Diversified by hill and wood,
   Down to the sea it stretched away.
I walked in paths our fathers trod.
   O'er verdant fields and flowery meads.
'Neath forest shades I pressed the sod.
   I wandered where each pathway leads.
Stately and grand before me rose

Clan Coffin's old ancestral home .
Our ancestors, in calm repose,
  For years have slumbered in the tomb.
Forgotten though their *names* on earth,
  In *deeds* their memory still survives :
Nantucket knows their honest worth,
  Now meets to eulogize their lives.
Assembled here a cultured crowd,
  No slander shall their lives defame :
" The Coffins fractious, noisy, loud,"
  Untruthful libel ! we proclaim.
Clan Coffin has, through every age,
  Kindly and true and faithful been.
Earnest and discreet, courageous, sage —
  This tribute to their lives we bring.

THE LAWS OF SIASCONSET.

A ballad proposed with a pipe of tobacco, as an evening's amusement to fisher-men. To the true Republicans of Siasconset, and to all who wish well to the cause of simplicity and plain dealing in society, one with another (which charac-terized the golden age of the ancients), this humble tribute is respectfully inscribed

BY PHILO-SIMPLICITAS.

WIDE in the East, on Nancy's Isle.
 Where roars the white surf louder.
Ascends to view the happy vill,
 For freedom famed, and chowder.
Fresh from the wave they take the cod,
 To feast the soul that wants it :
Its air is pure, its water good,
 Its name is Siasconset.

Old Saturn's reign is here begun,
 The Orient of the nations ;
Here kings and compliments are done,
 And all your Boston fashions.

The song, the jest, the smile serene
　　Amuse the friend that haunts it ;
Here old simplicity is seen,
　　In ancient dress, at 'Sconset.

Its pump the lymph oblivious pours,
　　To drown despite and treason :
Its purer air at once restores
　　To liberty and reason.
When erring virtue asks excuse,
　　'T is free good-nature grants it,
And that which else would be abuse
　　Is wink'd by laws of 'Sconset.

And should your fault incur a grudge,
　　Our court you must attend, sir :
Your Speaker 's Conscience : Reason, Judge :
　　Your Jury is a friend, sir.
This court guards well our dearest rights,
　　And when the country owns it,
Lawyers will starve with all their wits,
　　And curse the laws of 'Sconset.

Hygeia here her reign resumes,
    The hyp'd and crazy healing,
Restores old wounds, dispels the glooms,
    And brings the callous feelings.
Then let religious maniacs prate,
    And on the treaty bounce it.
Here invalids in church and state
    Are all made whole at 'Sconset.

The mind with priestcraft long beguiled
    May choose, with freedom handy,
Good Moses with the Spirit fill'd,
    Or Thomas Paine with brandy,
And thus will I, though pope and sect,
    With bulls and zeal denounce it :
My reason 's mine to think and act,
    Like thee, friend Siasconset.

The souls of once too rude a form
    Receive a softer moulding :
Here Jacobins forget to storm,
    And wives leave off their scolding.

POEMS OF NANTUCKET.

The wight in town, who swells with pride,
   Or like Clesippus vaunts it,
The paltry coxcomb lays aside,
   And wears the man at 'Sconset

Should party zeal the bosom rile,
   'T is here nor felt nor seen, sir.
For chowder well corrects the bile,
   And dissipates the spleen, sir.
Then, when with B**k the wild heart swells,
   Some genius bids renounce it,
For no revenge nor malice dwells
   With thee, O Siasconset.

Now, let the fair one share her part,
   Sweet village, in thy candor,
Safe to disclose her feeling heart,
   Nor fear the scorpion, slander.
Thus the fond maid shall find excuse,
   If first she makes the onset :
Her soul's elect her hand may choose
   By laws of Siasconset.

Should polygons and catspaws ask
    My judgment of the Vi'lence.
This law I'll claim to wear the mask,
    And answer them in silence.
Thrice happy vill, extend thy reign,
    Till every nation owns it ;
Thus shall the world its glory gain
    Beneath thy laws, O 'Sconset.

AT 'SCONSET, ON LEAVING

BY WILLIAM C. RICHARDS.

COULD ye but know, ye jealous mists that twine
   Your silvery scarfs around the sun and sea
To hide one long, last glimpse of both from me.
With what rare splendor sea and sun would shine
Through your rent veils, O vision half divine.
In filmy shreds and tatters, ye would flee.
Intoxicate with new-born vanity
Of conscious beauty in each fleeting line!

Then should I love your vapory forms of light.
Which now on 'Sconset's brow like shadows brood.
And vague and vain my straining glances make.
Avaunt, ye ghostly phantoms of the night!
My chiding verse should bless ye, if ye would.
Ah, Benedicite! Your flight ye take!

WITH A NANTUCKET SHELL.*

BY CHARLES HENRY WEBB.

I SEND thee a shell from the ocean beach;
But listen thou well, for my shell hath speech.
    Hold to thine ear,
    And plain thou 'lt hear
      Tales of ships
      That were lost in the rips,
    Or that sunk on shoals
    Where the bell-buoy tolls,
And ever and ever its iron tongue rolls
In a ceaseless lament for the poor lost souls.

    And a song of the sea
    Has my shell for thee:
    The melody in it
    Was hummed at Wauwinet,
    And caught at Coatue
    By the gull that flew
Outside to the ship with its perishing crew.

* By permission of Harper Bros

POEMS OF NANTUCKET

But the white wings wave
Where none may save,
And there's never a stone to mark a grave

See! its sad heart bleeds
For the sailor's needs:
But it bleeds again
For more mortal pain.
More sorrow and woe,
Than is theirs who go,
With shuddering eyes and whitening lips,
Down in the sea on their shattered ships.

Thou fearest the sea?
Ah, a tyrant is he —
A tyrant as cruel as tyrant may be:
But though winds fierce blow,
And the rocks lie low,
And the coast be lee,
This I say to thee:
Of Christian souls more have been wrecked on shore
Than ever were lost at sea.

NANTUCKET, AUG. 15, 1881.

MEETING AND PARTING.

BY MARIA L. OWEN,

FROM THE GERMAN OF LENAU.

WHENE'ER she came, her form appeared to me
Lovely as the first green that veils the tree

And when she spoke, seemed to my heart her words
Sweet as the earliest song of woodland birds.

And when her gentle hand waved me adieu.
It seemed as if my youth's last dream went too.